It's near
and the coun

DECEMBER

X	2	3	4	5	6	7
8	9	10	11	12	13	14
15	16	17	18	19	20	21
22	23	24	25	26	27	28
29	30	31				

Find the flaps on every page.

Some ride a sled down the hill and other boys and girls go skating. Animals walk through frosty leaves.

CRUNCH
CRUNCH

A Christmas Advent Story

Ivy Snow

illustrated by Hannah Tolson

BLOOMSBURY
CHILDREN'S BOOKS
NEW YORK LONDON OXFORD NEW DELHI SYDNEY

Christmas cards come through your door, and snowflakes start to fall.

WOOF WOOF

1

Wrap up in your
scarves and hats,
and pull your boots on.

4

5

Who is hiding behind the tree?

Look inside the Christmas shops
and see what you can find. Ballerinas
spin and twirl while drummers beat
a festive sound.

THE TOY SHOP

No. 6

What else is in the window?

SHOES & HATS

the DELI

the DELI

Glittery lights
shine in the street.

7

DING DING

Christmas trees are all around. Big ones
and bushy ones, tall ones and
thin ones, decorated with colorful
twinkling lights.

Some are sprinkled with shiny icicles.
How many can you count?

9

TWEET TWEET

Sing carols in a wintry
square loud for all to hear.
The stars are sparkling
in the sky. Can you spot
the moon?

10

TRA LA LA LA LA

Who is on the hill?

11

Decorate the Christmas tree with
ornaments,
lights,
and ribbons.

13

What other decorations will you find?
An angel, reindeer, dove, or owl?
There's one of every kind!

14

TWIT TWOO

Wrap your presents with spots and stripes and other Christmas patterns.

15

Put them underneath the tree.

It's not long until they'll be opened.

Bake lots of yummy cookies to share with all your friends.

Ice them and eat them,

wrap them and give them,

or hang them on the tree.

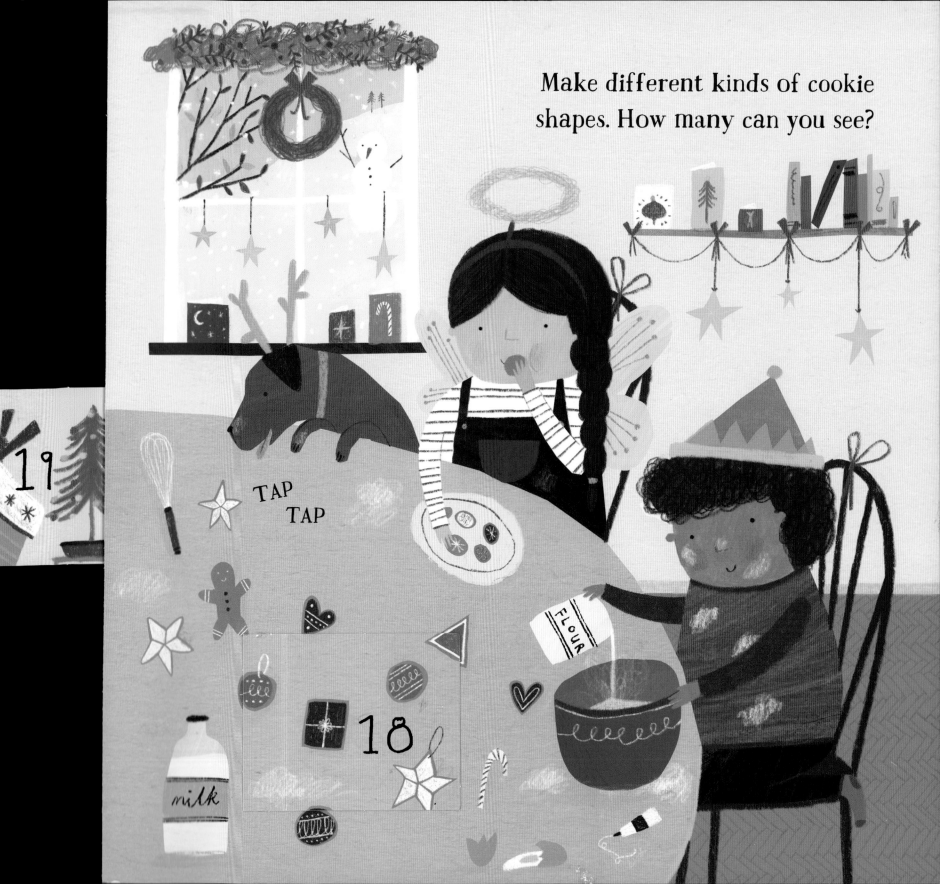

Make different kinds of cookie shapes. How many can you see?

TAP
TAP

It's snowing outside on Christmas Eve,
and everyone is quiet. The stars
are out, and we're all in bed.

Lamp

But who will visit you in the night?

An elf,
a reindeer?

SHHHHH

20

21

Or even Santa in his sleigh?

Hooray! It's Christmas day!

What has Santa brought you? What will you find under the tree?

Wear Christmas hats, and open presents joyfully.

23

YIPPEE

BLOOMSBURY CHILDREN'S BOOKS
Bloomsbury Publishing Inc., part of Bloomsbury Publishing Plc
1385 Broadway, New York, NY 10018

BLOOMSBURY, BLOOMSBURY CHILDREN'S BOOKS, and the Diana logo
are trademarks of Bloomsbury Publishing Plc

First published in Great Britain in October 2017 by Bloomsbury Publishing Plc
Published in the United States of America in September 2018
by Bloomsbury Children's Books

Bloomsbury books may be purchased for business or promotional use. For information on bulk purchases please contact
Macmillan Corporate and Premium Sales Department at specialmarkets@macmillan.com

Library of Congress Cataloging-in-Publication Data
Names: Snow, Ivy, author. | Tolson, Hannah, illustrator.
Title: A Christmas Advent story / by Ivy Snow ; illustrated by Hannah Tolson.
Description: New York : Bloomsbury, 2018.
Summary: Snow is falling on Christmas Eve, the stars are out, and everyone is in bed—will Santa visit in the night? Follow the story
of a little girl, a boy, and their dog in this advent countdown. Along the way you'll find 25 flaps, each introducing a new word.
Identifiers: LCCN 2018010840
ISBN 978-1-68119-851-4 (hardcover)
Subjects: LCSH: Lift-the-flap books—Specimens.
Classification: LCC PZ7.1.S657343 Chr 2018 | DDC [E]—dc23
LC record available at https://lccn.loc.gov/2018010840

Art created digitally
Typeset in Mrs Ant
Book design by Sophie Gordon
Printed in China by Leo Paper Products, Heshan, Guangdong
2 4 6 8 10 9 7 5 3 1

All papers used by Bloomsbury Publishing Plc are natural, recyclable products made from wood grown in well-managed forests.
The manufacturing processes conform to the environmental regulations of the country of origin.

To find out more about our authors and books visit www.bloomsbury.com and sign up for our newsletters.